For Selkie Doak

SELKIE

Josephine Birch

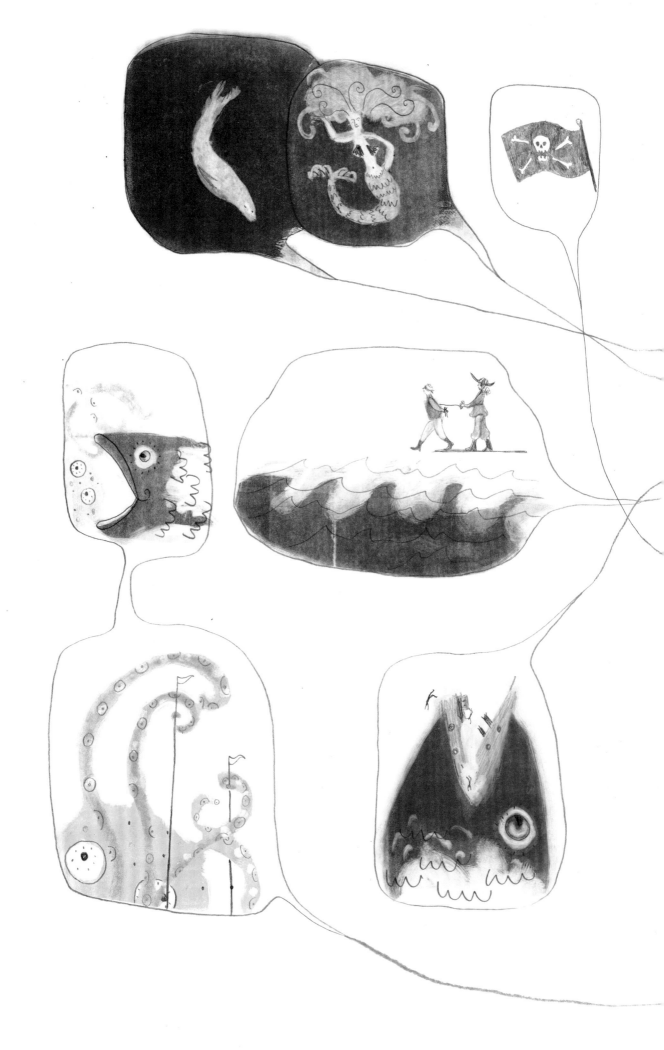

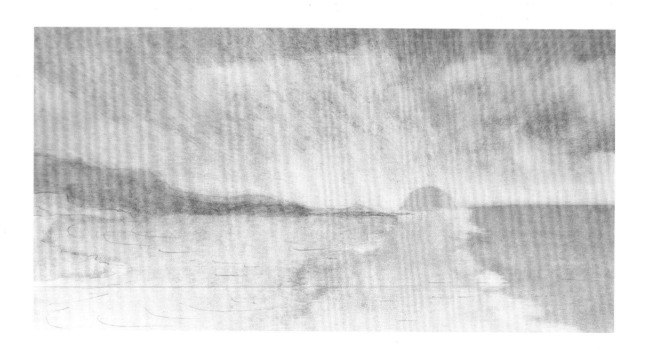

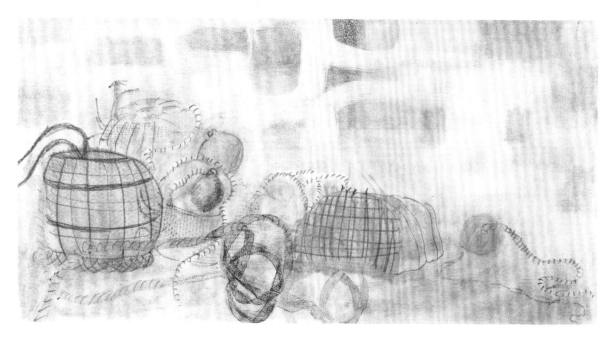

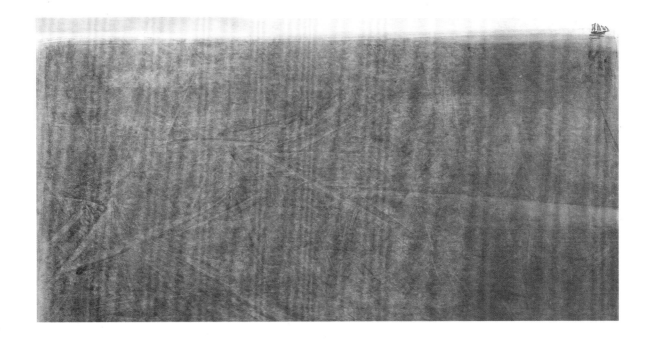

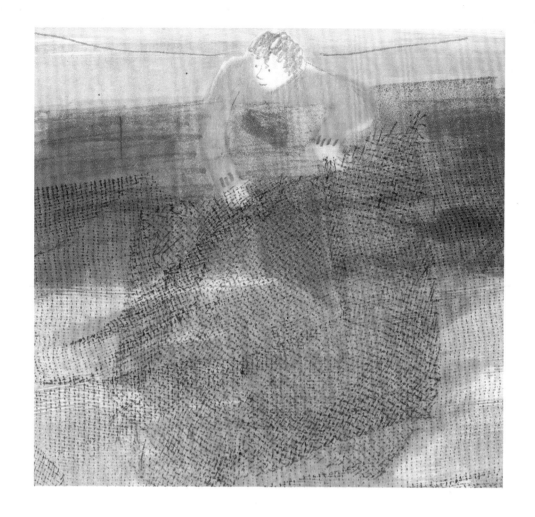

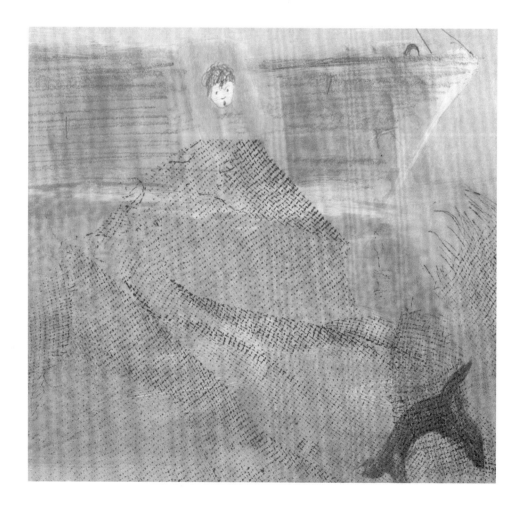

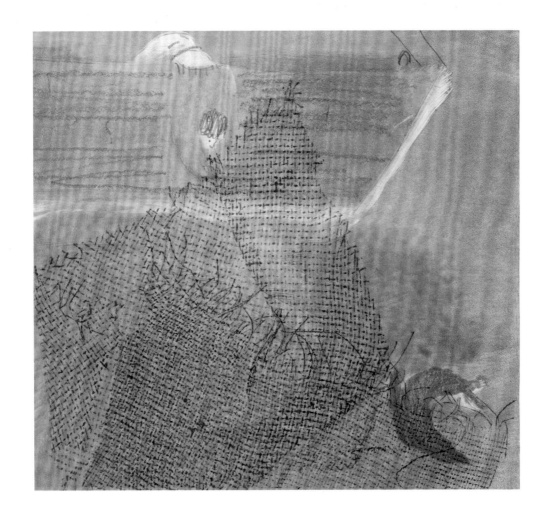

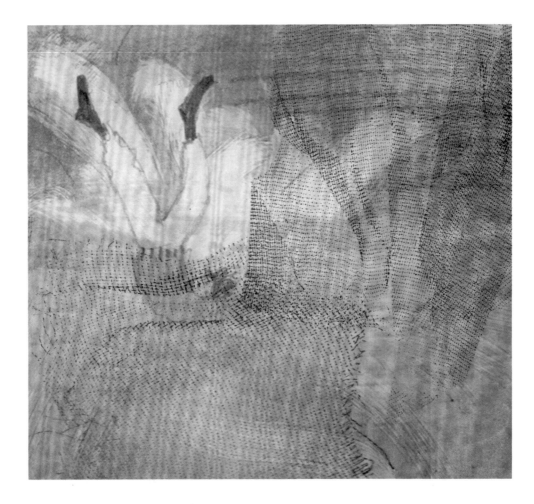

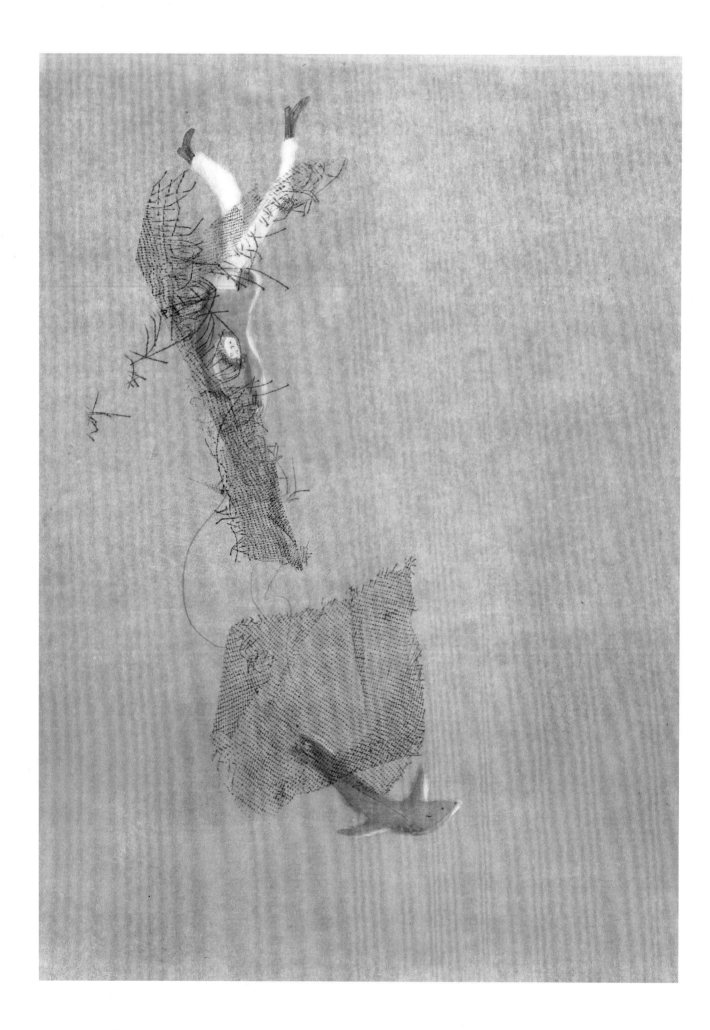

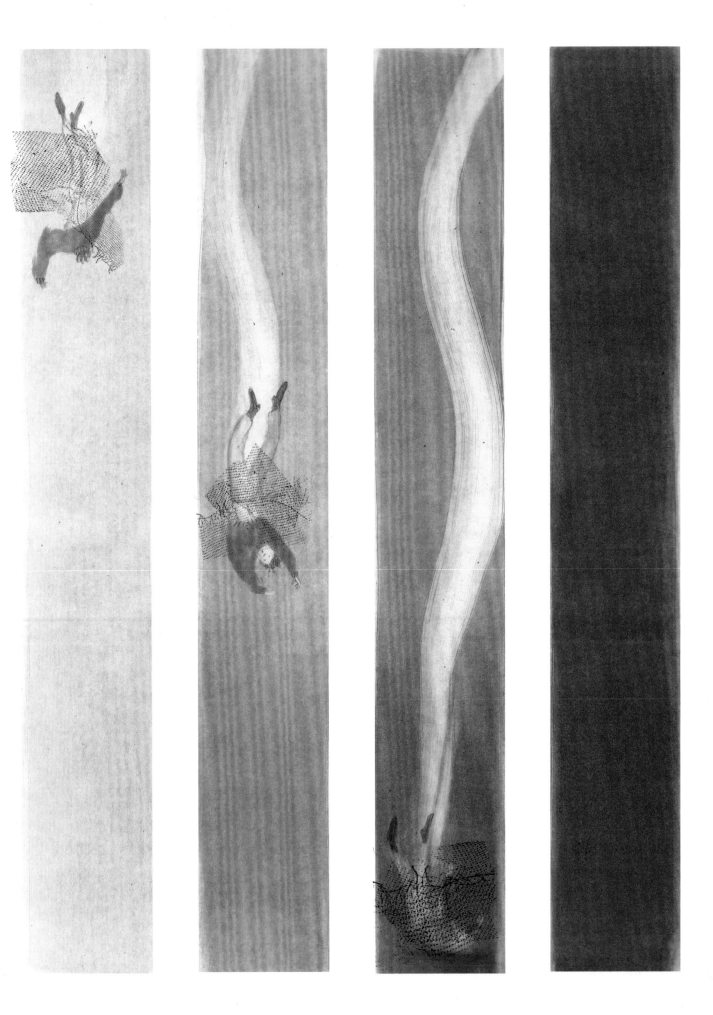

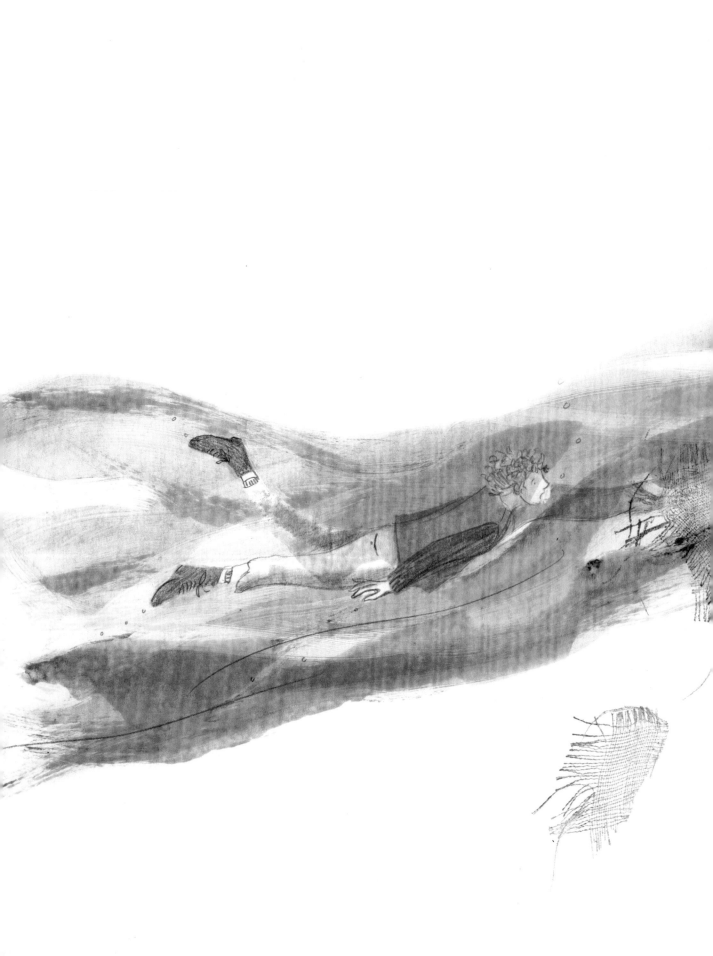

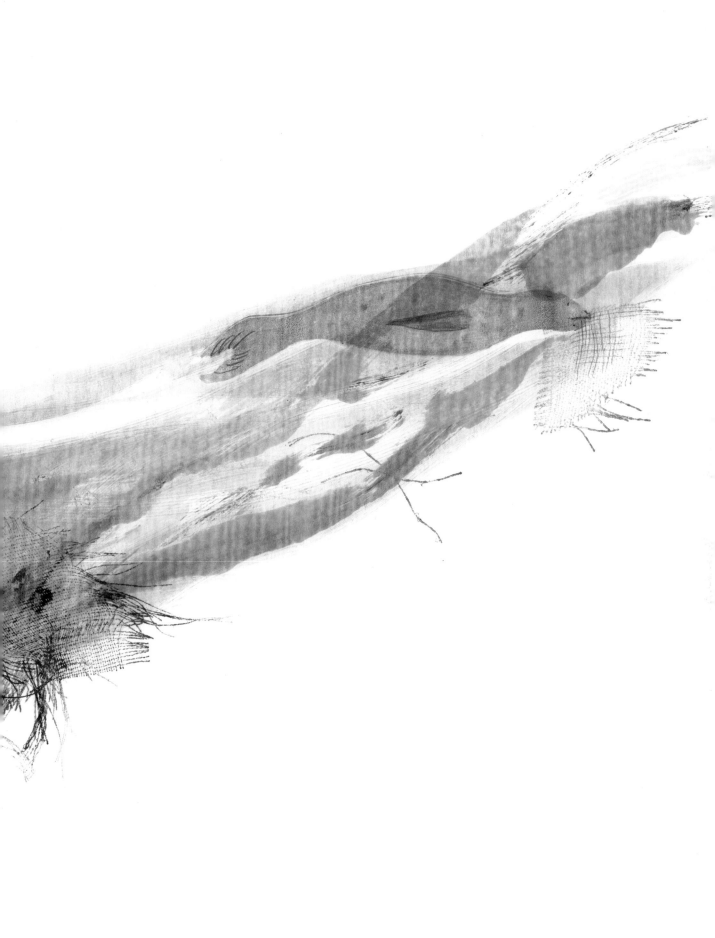

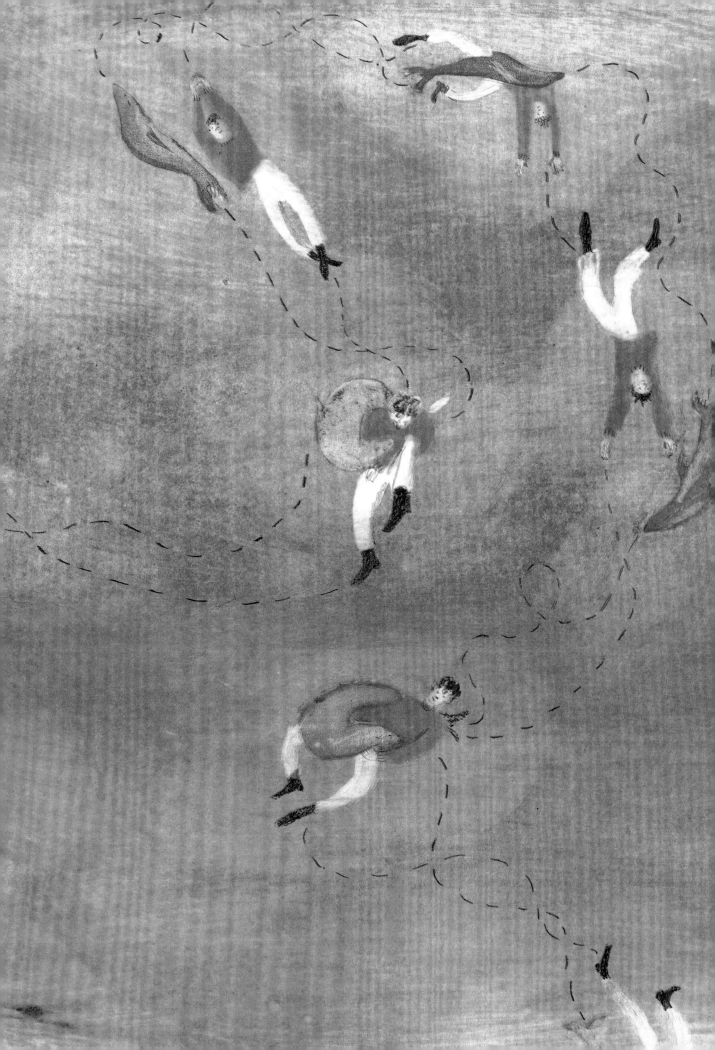

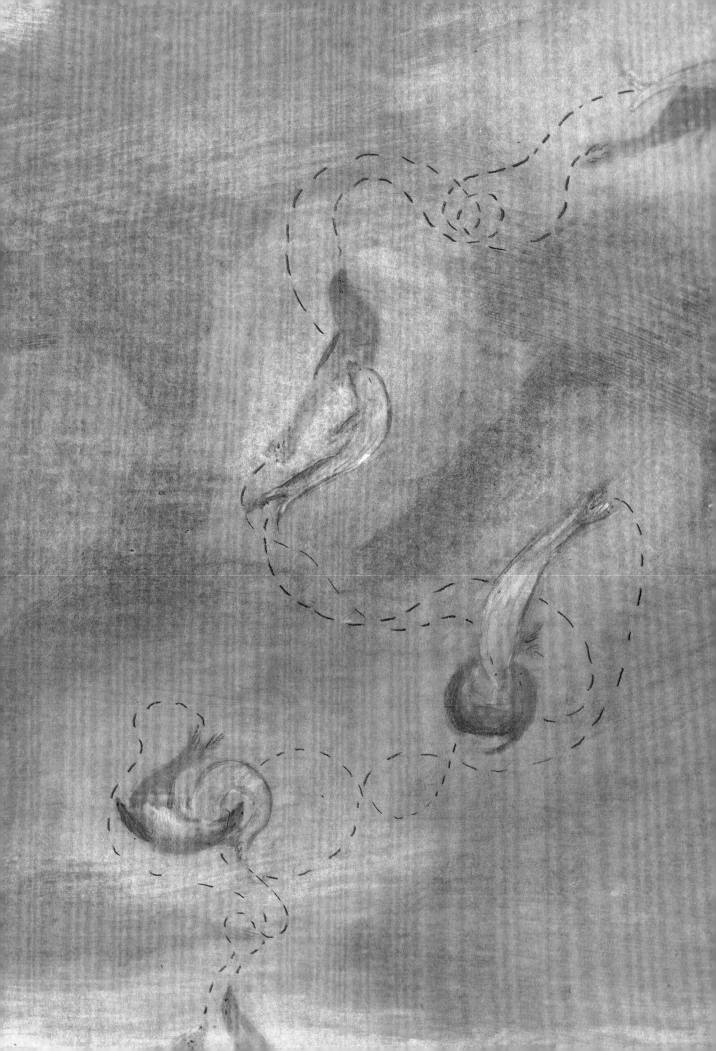

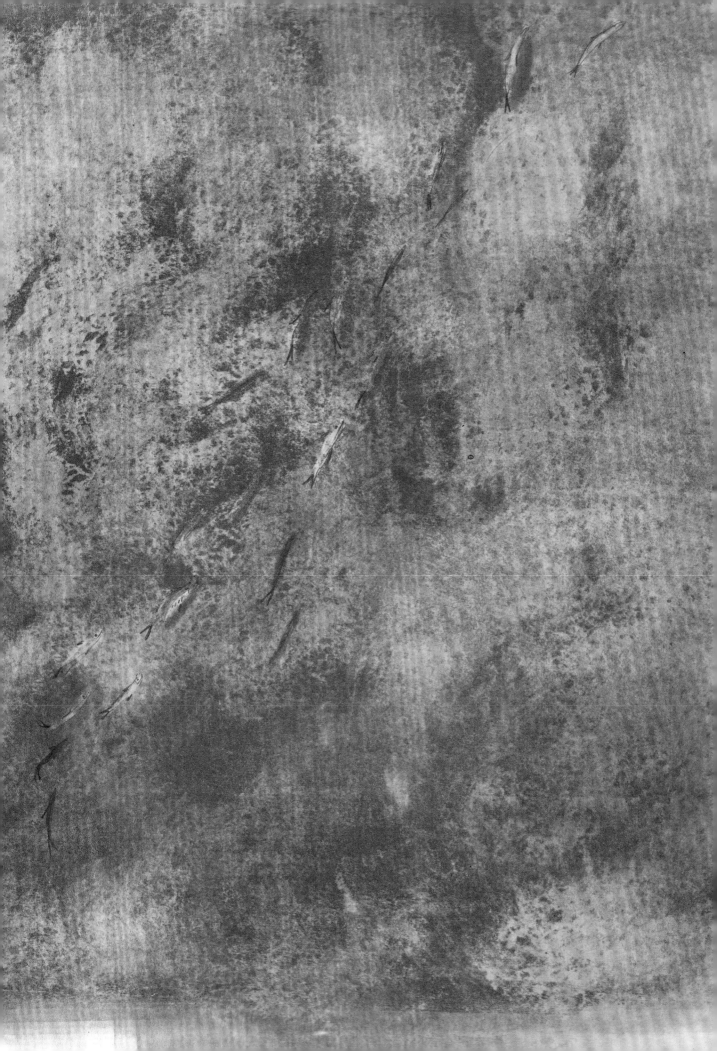

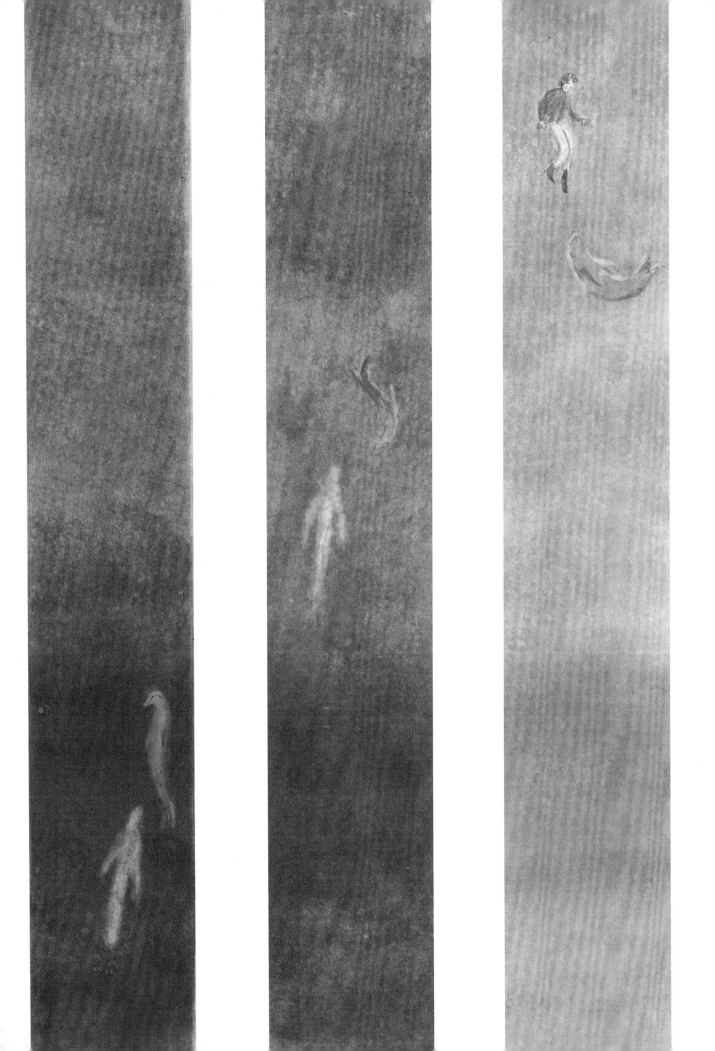

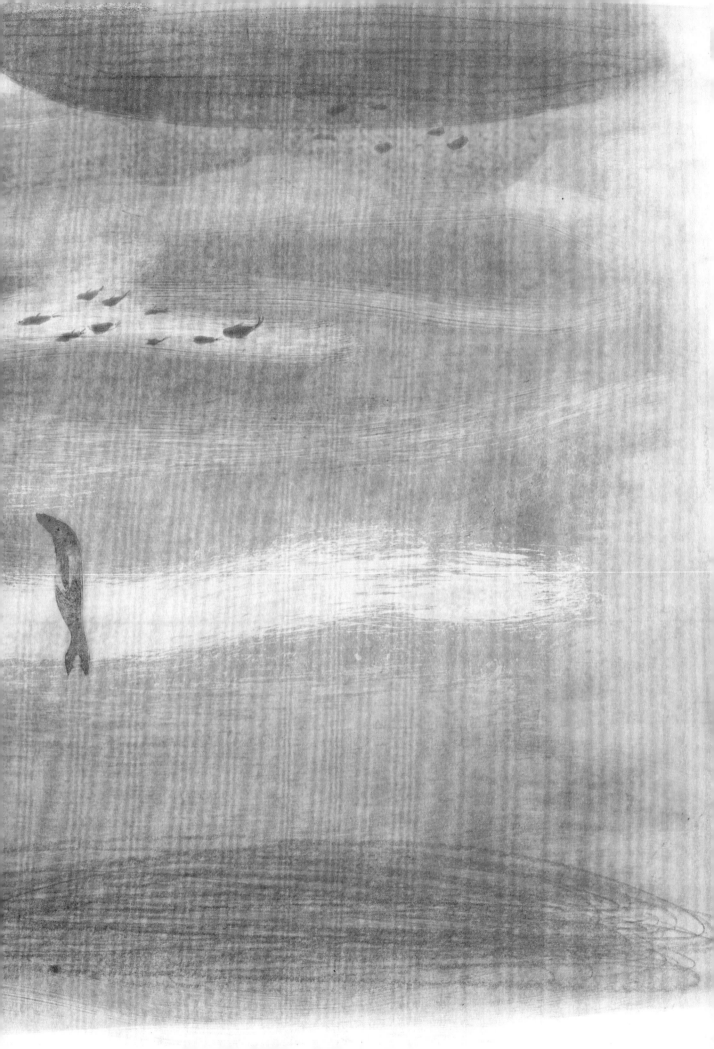

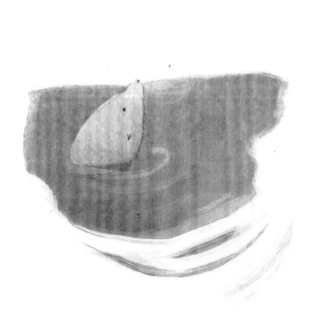

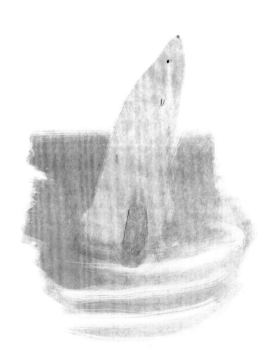

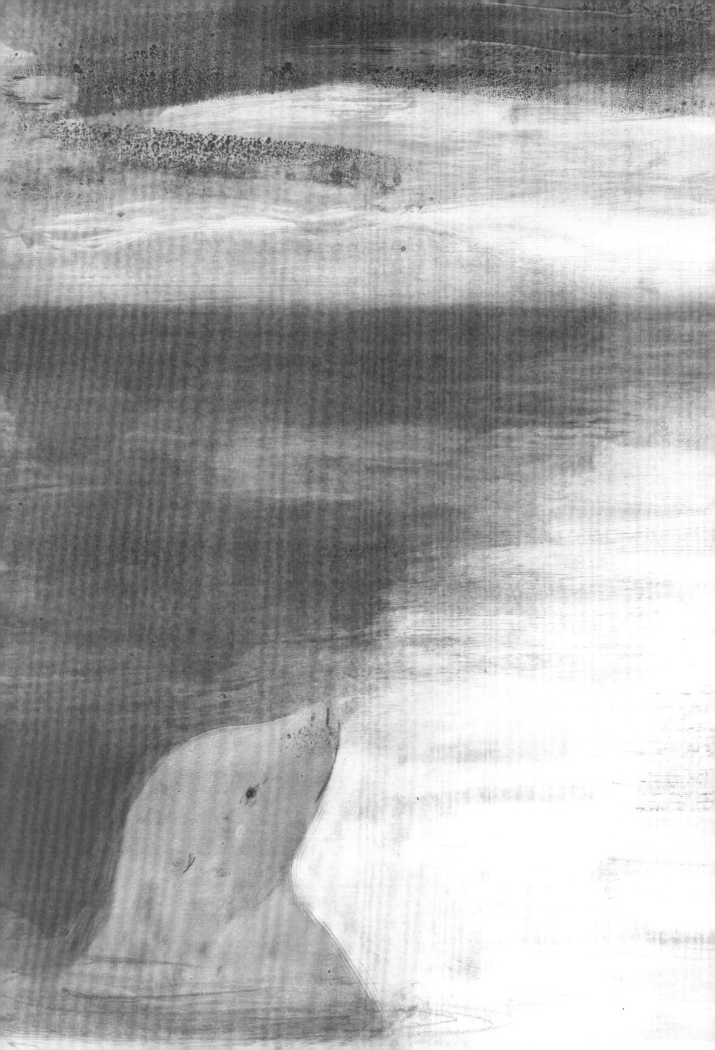

Starfish Bay® Children's Books
An imprint of Starfish Bay Publishing
www.starfishbaypublishing.com

SELKIE

© Josephine Birch, 2019
ISBN 978-1-76036-054-2
First Published 2019
Printed in China by Beijing Shangtang Print & Packaging Co., Ltd.
11 Tengren Road, Niulanshan Town, Shunyi District, Beijing, China

Josephine Birch studied a Bachelor of Arts in Illustration at the Cambridge School of Art and on the 'Drawing Year' scholarship at The Royal Drawing School, London. Her Master of Arts in Children's Book Illustration was obtained from the Cambridge School of Art. Josephine grew up in the South West of England, in a tiny terraced house with a garden. The garden was full of flowers, vegetables, and home to chickens, two tortoises, a naughty dog and an old bath full of goldfish and lilies. Her mother, a dress maker and teacher, and her older sister, a painter, made the house a colourful and creative place to live. Josephine always knew she wanted to work as an artist and with animals. Through her studies, Josephine discovered that she could combine the two by illustrating stories inspired by the natural world and her favourite animals.

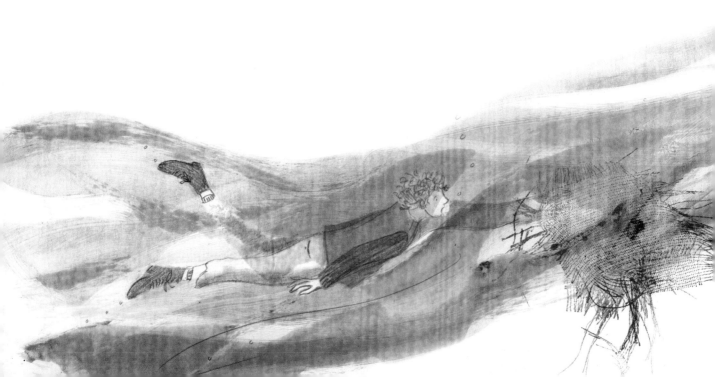

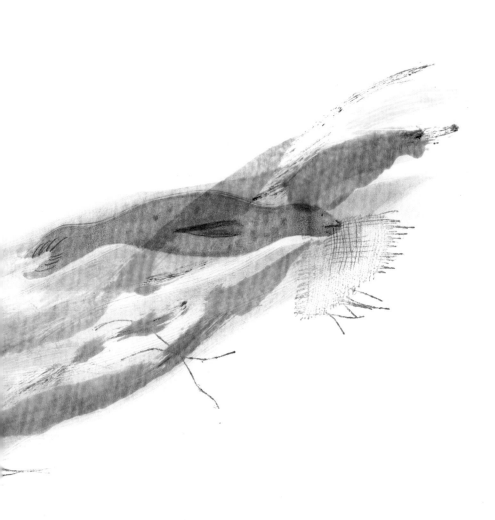